The Illiterate Ghost

(Fictions of Fear, Absurdity and Madness)

Alan Price

The Illiterate Ghost by Alan Price

ISBN: 978-1-908125-91-0

Cover Art by David Rix

Publication Date: October 2019

All text copyright 2019 Alan Price.

Some of these fictions have been published in the magazines The Delinquent, The Recusant, Flash, I love you! (Paper Swans Press Anthology-2018), The Wednesday and one at alanprice69.wordpress.com/

To Bob Quaif

Contents

An Agent's Description of Home

The lift's operation is impeccable. In the event of a challenge, speak to the concierge. He's an obedient man, eager to please. Your apartment is perfectly secure and double glazed as thick as a bank-vault door though allowing a certain transparency. Noise has been replaced by the idea of noise. I'm confident you can prosper in this desolate yet picturesque part of the city.

The kitchen is alive with equipment, though unlikely to be used. For we ask you to continue eating out: fine cuisine will be served in our neighbouring hotel. But we've provided a freezer and microwave for the limited amusement of breakfast. And our air conditioning is perfectly pitched to erase all memory of those recent heatwaves, so unpleasant for working.

We've endeavoured to give you a bed that will digitally massage your body before sleep takes you off. The execution of deep-sleeping is taken very seriously. It must be balanced with your deep-working. Our clients stay for a night or a weekend, resting content on specially scented pillows next to their i-phones and tablets. When suitably refreshed, you will move on to meet further customers.

It's important to remember that no apartment is intended to be a fixed locatable spot but more a blurred snapshot or a smudged mark on a map. Our changeable rooms (like moveable feasts) are intended to deflect the homing instinct. Any thoughts about creating a domesticity styled to your own taste are to be avoided at all cost. You are here to be a light cloud passing through an otherwise clear blue sky.

Panic attacks, you say? Certainly, they can be accommodated. Our most driven workers ask us to remove all furniture and fittings, save for their bed. The more minimal the room, the less the distraction: leaving the mind prepared to achieve its breaking point. A panic room can be arranged within twenty-four hours.

Three months' rent is payable in advance, excluding the rare occasion when you invite a client to have drinks in the lounge. Then we charge for the entertaining of guests, who must be vetted beforehand. They cannot stay overnight. Any prolonging of company is prohibited. That would be a patch of grey on your busy cloud.

For a more detailed description of the whole of the building, please consult our information pack. This is available in all the appropriate business languages. You may read it later. All that concerns us now is the signing of the contract. After careful examination, the loyalty and acuity of your own work-site was found to be responsive to our blue sky. I trust that you will be productive and happily develop, with us.

The Keeper of Frankenstein

In May 2005 Arnold G. Decker, a stubborn film collector, who possessed a print of the believed lost 1910 film *Frankenstein* made by Edison Studios, died aged eighty-four, in his neatly arranged, if grimy, bathroom in Weed Ground, a suburb of Fort Worth, Texas. His daughter and son in law were sad, but not surprised, when informed by the police that the recluse's body, unnoticed for a month, had badly decomposed.

Decker had lobbied the Academy of Arts and Sciences for millions of dollars and an Oscar in recognition of his saving of *Frankenstein*. The guardians of the academy said no, but offered him a pittance for one of their few surviving 'children' of early American cinema. In response, Decker acted like a tyrannical Victorian parent. He locked his Frankenstein in a cupboard and waited.

The creature of the deteriorating film was so shocked on looking into a mirror that it vanished. Frankenstein arrived. In the mirror, he saw the monster's image as his own image. The creature disappeared leaving Frankenstein with his own reflection. Frankenstein's fiancée entered the room and warmly embraced him. Afterwards, the final inter-title read *The creation of an evil mind is overcome by love and disappears.*

One day, Decker decided to open the cupboard and go public with his find. A home-made video was struck and a DVD was burnt. Decker's name was scrawled across every frame of *Frankenstein* as if he were its creator. Decker dressed up as Old Father Time and left home to attended film collector fairs. But his *Frankenstein* 'child' didn't appeal as expected and he became neither rich nor famous.

Arnold G. Decker, before dying in your bath, didn't you realise that you were fated to be a mean collector of old films: chosen to save Frankenstein from being melted down for its meagre silver content? Before closing your eyes, did this creation, of the Edison Manufacturing Company, reveal itself to you?

Frankenstein's creature should have kicked your arse and set you on the road to act responsibly – been a loving companion and allowed the movie authorities to restore its thingness; satisfy a hungry audience waiting in the dark. Instead you held on to an unhappy bandaged creature. We might have praised you, Decker. You could have looked into the bathroom mirror and only seen your purified self.

Index to the 1896/1907 Films of Georges Méliès

(A Cut Up Fiction)

1000 feet of silent film = 15 minutes

Ten ladies we are, in one umbrella, playing cards, waiting at Joinville station for the arrival of a train. Oh what a nightmare was our holiday, such a fantastical subject! A Peeping Tom at the seaside, with Chopin's Funeral March Burlesqued, tried to engage us in a fat and lean wrestling match. Thank goodness for the arrival of the hat with many surprises. Out popped the skipping cheeses smelling like phantasmal vapours.

Who looks, pays! we shouted hurling ourselves from the cabinet, quite bewildering Bob Kick the mischievous kid, a powerful conjuror with a hundred tricks. Yet we Ten Ladies (making ten hats in sixty seconds) led him a serpentine dance under the seas. From out of the infernal cauldron, the weather changed and the beach at Villiers was in gale.

The Monster was struck by the invisible Siva. Ah, Beelzebub's daughters couldn't have done better! A rogue's tricks were halted. Satan was now in prison.

At the Academy for Young ladies, we'll be applauded. Why what is this? The Czar and his Cortege going to Versailles are on the platform. Will the Palace of the Arabian Nights entice? Shall he grant us an impossible voyage back home?

Targets

Alex, a home improvements sales rep, went on holiday after only realising forty-six per cent of his 'potential' sales. He was warned to make quality and customer satisfaction a singular obsession. His young micro-managing colleagues told him to fight harder to achieve his targets.

On holiday, Alex worried. *Work harder. Don't be bored with life. Work harder for less.* was the mantra he texted to himself. Oiled customers, tapping his company's app, sprawled by the hotel lobby, restaurant and swimming pool, gave him no peace. Alex kept seeing everyone as an unrealised percentage. On his return flight, he even counted the passengers, but failed to make his target.

By the taxi-ramp people kept running up to him. Yet Alex's numbers were still not enough. Arriving home, he discovered more work assembled inside his garage. He was pleased that fifty-four men, and women, had managed to comfortably fit in there.

Now things added up. Alex carefully attached a hosepipe to his car exhaust. They watched his every move, whispered and made notes. The anxious crowd only backed off and walked away after Alex expired from monoxide poisoning.

The coroner concluded that there was more to life than business plans and a constant striving for profit. Yet if Alex had attended his own inquest, he would have disagreed; stood up, offered his hosepipe, like a comforting vape, to the coroner and probably said, *I subscribed to the ideals of the company and betrayed my customers. Now my home improvements are bereft. I'm ashamed. Look about you and see. Here are the spirit percentages of the lost fifty-four!*

At the Back
of Burlesque

The dark-haired woman, in the short orange dress, performed many duties. She waited in a corner of the club, hovered around customers, escorted you to your table and asked a waiter to bring the menu. And when, as if by magic, the waiters disappeared, was left alone to administer the wine tasting. It was a ritual she enjoyed.

That evening there was a problem opening a bottle of red wine. The women, at the table, were already sipping their white. The men prayed for the release of an obdurate wine cork. They sensed Miss Orange's struggle. She gave them a fraught smile. They were startled by the cry of a female compere. It was synchronised with the wine's release from its tight neck. Their hostess poured the wine. The men sipped, pretending to savour it, glanced at their partners, and nodded in approval. Miss Orange filled their glasses.

The compere approached. She was a formidable diva wearing a titanic brown wig and inhabiting a red jewelled sequined dress. From her sartorial fortress, she began her temptation routine.

After her jokes and once a man, selected from the closest table, had been sat upon, she threw her shawl to the back of the stage. Seconds before the start, the orange hostess's arm could be glimpsed, in the semi-darkness, removing the diva's shawl.

The first act was a stripper, flimsily dressed in blue, doing an obvious blue routine. Each bit of clothing was skilfully thrown aside. The mistress of orange adroitly entered to pick up all things blue. Hardly had she clutched them to her chest, when the presenter reappeared to tell more jokes and 'humiliate' further customers. Meanwhile an obese second stripper, dressed in a white Marie Antoinette costume, waited anxiously behind the curtain. The young woman got in the stripper's way. Marie glared at her servant, this mere table-top hostess.

Antoinette entered to strip to her corset and reveal a plastic container of slimming tablets. Moaning of her 'large prison of fat', she stuffed her mouth with tablets, and began to playfully spit them out over the audience. Now only wearing a g-string and tassels on her nipples, Antoinette cupped her formidable breasts. Then she threw the remainder of the tablets onto the floor where they were stamped underfoot. Marie Antoinette left the stage for her fan, a box of tissues and a cold beer. The orange hostess, holding a small pan and brush, cleared up. The tablets (really polystyrene pellets), were swept into a plastic bag. The diva compere re-emerged. No customer 'insults'. No more jokes. She sat at her piano and began to sing *Just one more for the road.*

For the young orange hostess, there was still more work, another hour of table service, cork removal and brushing up. Then could she exchange her dress for jeans and top, and taxi back home. Yet for a moment, by the back of the burlesque stage, she temporarily forgot that she was a hard-up student. She became, through her menial duties, an orange butterfly of provocation and innocence. A service provided, or paraded by her different beauty, that worked on – swift, exact and unnoticed.

The Illiterate Ghost

Audrey Finnegan, a twenty-year-old factory worker who lived in Swiss Cottage, London, was murdered by her boyfriend Marcus Touchstone, a twenty-five-year-old unemployed actor. It happened during the bitterly cold winter of 1962. The couple had been to the cinema to see *Yield to the Night,* a fifties film, starring Diana Dors, a leading British actress of that time. The 'blonde bombshell', minus her make-up, starred in a grim prison drama where she's hung for killing her lover.

Walking back home to Touchstone's bed-sit, they made a detour through a building site covered in deep snow. The film proved depressing and triggered an argument about their relationship. Audrey stopped and mentioned some nasty gossip, about Diana Dors, that she'd read in her copy of *The News of the World.* Marcus pulled the newspaper out of his girlfriend's coat pocket. It wasn't true. Audrey had lied. She confessed that she couldn't read or write and had said those things just to annoy him. Marcus, who lived on a schizoid edge, exploded and strangled her.

Kneeling over her corpse, he recited Rosalyn's sharp sexual advice to Phoebe, in *As You Like It*. "Sell when you can, you are not for all markets." He wept as he threw Audrey into the deep pit, dug out for the new library, finished off his hip flask of brandy and walked home. Three days later, Touchstone was arrested on suspicion of murder. He broke down and confessed. Before they placed a rope around his neck, he cried out an odd re-working of Shakespeare's lines. "Read and write, when you can do Audrey. Now, you are not for all markets."

In 2002, Nancy, a library assistant, was in the basement shelving books when she saw a young woman bending over a trolley. It wasn't a colleague. Nancy thought it was a member of the public who'd come down by mistake. Audrey Finnegan, dressed in her snow-covered overcoat, opened books, glanced at a few pages then threw them to the ground. Frustrated she cried out for Marcus to help her. Nancy ran back upstairs.

A year later, when re-furbishing the old basement, a builder discovered, jammed behind a radiator, a complete works of Shakespeare bookmarked by a copy of *The News of the World*. He still says, to this day, that on opening it a man whispered in his ear "Diana Dors wasn't a hunter in my market. Forgive me, Audrey. Forgive me!"

Swimmer

Whenever I'm swimming, I have a dread of being hit by another swimmer, especially from the back. A clammy sense of someone's propelled hands and feet striking very hard, and very directed, against my thighs and lower back. A head-on collision's more likely, but here my fear can be deflected, assuming there's time to get out of the way. It's more the not knowing who, or what, is behind you till they touch, scratch and dig in. It's difficult to turn round, if you dare, and look them in the eye. Like some fiend with a frightful tread, out of Coleridge's albatross world, wanting to press down on its prey, my malevolent swimmer pursues me. Maybe, such a swimmer is pursuing all of us. From the pre-birth waters to our safe and supposed dry land of life, we are stalked. I'm trying not to look back to find out.

Swimmers do their crawl, backstroke, breaststroke, even butterfly. They swim indifferent to me, ignoring my presence. Or are they? Are their exercises a preliminary form of attack? Take the lanes we all swim in – or try to. They quickly become overcrowded. Slow, medium and fast lanes. A slow speed in a fast lane is suicide (a kind of watery equivalent of smashing your car on the motorway for not keeping up). Medium lane is best if you are slow, but not too slow. Things are tolerated till the stronger medium swimmers' snap back – like piranhas. As for using the slow lane itself – well, this can be very slow indeed. Here, you become a medium creature always having to be careful of collisions, timing and adjustment of pace. If not, the over-slow ones resent you and get angry. There's a real danger of a group gathering. I don't want that. Beaten by a crowd, who carry me, ceremoniously, alive or dead, to an unknown swimming lane.

I've done twenty-four lengths now. Six left. Today there's a Jamaican man, with dreadlocks, looking like an octopus hat, swimming faster than me. Suddenly he plunges underwater. I'm scared that, like a submarine, he will then rapidly ascend so as to hit my chest head-on. But I've just seen his legs. So little, under his long beach shorts. The legs look bitten, broken off. Now I realise they're only stumps. Must have been shaped in his pre-birth waters, or else the medium swimmers got to him. I feel contrite, ashamed and stupid. Ready to forgive. But now, offgaurd, he hits me hard and down I go. I flounder helpless, losing all memory of how to swim. I sink into myself, as if a dull stone were drowning. Is it pleasure, or is it pain? Surely the bold swimmer, the watching one, in front us, on the broken platform, has to wake up, dive in and save me?

I Need to Fly or 2½ Days in Tashkent, 1990

My Icarus wings and Icarus hopes are packed in the baggage hold. The plane has broken down en route, London – Prague – Kabul - Delhi. Detoured to a strange land. I'm trapped in a Tashkent hotel lobby. Cracked walls. Work dust. Bag of cement. A pile of Russian bricks. Buzzing fly. Glut of guests forming a queue. Dejected faces. Hotel clerk barking, atonal. *In Hotel Muscovy, you do not answer back!* My room has holes in the walls. Black and white TV. Chopin piano competition. A polonaise competes with the whistling wind. Radiator gasping. Dirty windows. Room overlooking wide streets, where Tashkentians shuffle through an icy mush.

My stomach rumbles for lunch. Descent in the lift. Small framed men in badly cut suits, wearing pork-pie hats and clutching videos. In wall-to-wall mirrors, they chatter and multiply. Lift hits the ground. Some exit for the games room to press their grubby hands against pinball machines. Others enter a blue-lit room beating out a desperate cabaret.

I head for the restaurant. Slavic arms of muscular chav women. Ladling a soup trying to drown the sad carrot in your bowl. Dropping in chunks of bread with a rind called cheese. My ingested carrot begins to chase the onion in my stomach.

I fly to the hotel exit and greet an Afghan army officer. He takes me to a beaten up car, then a battered taxi. Grand opening of cash box. My five pound note gleefully swapped for roubles. We drive to the street market. Kilo of earthy apples. Tea. Cakes. Grinning boy with samovar.

Back at the hotel, a bald sniffing man stands by the games room. Tashkent airport rep. Bereft of a plane. Heavy snow in Kabul. No flying today. He weeps, blowing his nose with a batik handkerchief. Russian hotel clerk covers her face, to ward off any Soviet satellite germs. The lift is broken. I climb the stairs, now more absent of stair rods. A mysterious turd has been left by my door.

Party raging till 3am. Banging of many doors. A knocking hits my room. I open the door. Prostitute waving a pair of peacock feather fans. Then she reveals a multi-coloured condom. *Very good Tashkent girl. Cheap. Cheap. No germ aids!* If I could only steal her fans. Construct some flimsy wings. Or blow the condom into a balloon. Fly out of the room, away from her flesh, far from this noise, into the cold night sky.

Another day at the market. Kara Kelpecs, Asian Uzbeks, Mongols and Chinese. Explosion of hustling faces. A peep at a mosque. A peep at a broken pavement, just before I trip. Hurt and gazing at a department store window. Wanting to buy a silk cushion cover. No manager today. No key for the window. No sale. More earthy apples, plus free badges of Lenin, fail to compensate.

Silence tonight. The condom girl sleeps very tight. After breakfast, the rep returns shaking his hips. Almost dancing. Waving a fax. *The snow has melted. We can Kabul!* Small airport. Fractured steps. Entrance reeking of urine. Broken flight indicator boards. A huge stopped clock. Two plate glass doors. One shattered. Baggage piled up into an ugly hill. Customs declaration forms. No English copy. I guess at the Russian and always write NO. Bored soldiers. Sleepy drilled bureaucrats with eyes that never shut. *Perestroika. Glasnost.* Remember those words? No time for lunch. The military unblocks us. I sit on a freezing plane. Two unexplained hours of not taking off.

Oh give me back my freedom. Find me an Indian sun. Let me chose, by myself, how to fly once again. Unpack my suitcase, remove my

Icarus wings, unpack my reason. Unleash me onto the runway. Strap on the wax frame and feathers. Lift me off from this 'in transit' wreckage. *Let's Delhi! Let's Delhi! Let's Delhi!*

Space

He was told, in school, that life sprang from a burning pact with radiation that was later doused by the sea. Putting fire and water to one side, he thought that the last road for the disenchanted traveller might be space (once called the celestial sphere where God ran the show without the support of a NASA budget.).

Evangelical astronauts drove buggies and escorted well-heeled customers on their space-walking. But tourism gradually frightened him. People discussed real-estate and development. All he wanted was to be out all day, with his pick, gathering moon rocks and dreaming.

On the way back to Earth, a hatch was opened and he was thrown out for failing to toast the corporation. With champagne glass in hand, he hoped that gravity, in the form of a star or meteorite, wouldn't strike him. Before dying, he recalled that his great, great grandfather, when a child, had taken the book *The Young Traveller in Outer Space* out of the library and forgotten to return it.

What is a Praying Mantis?
(A Cut-Up Fiction for the Mantis Community)

With its head bowed and its arms folded, the praying mantis has the look of an insect worshipping. But it is rather a greedy insect and not at all merciful in its ways. It seizes its food with its shears, and bites its victim bit by bit. Sir J.A.Thompson says that, when it is feeding, it is like a schoolboy eating an apple, and between bites stopping to watch it getting less and less.

The Wonder Book of Tell Me Why (1935)

Sir J.A.Thompson has folded the insect i. Its schoolboy head and arms bowed with the look of an apple and is stopping to watch says its mantis. It is rather merciful in its ways. It bites at its food victim getting it less and less, bit by bit. It's not bites but a praying between feeding. And that when worshipping it seizes, eating greedy with its shears, and all is insect like.

Schoolboy eating the mantis apple has the praying look of an its Sir and it is its as bit by bit it seizes its greedy J.A.Thompson head and arms, to watch its folded in food, getting less between its shears. And with its feeding and victim bites stopping, is not at all less merciful but rather a bowed insect with its worshipping ways. When it bites like it says that's an It.

Letters for a Known Man

I'm startled when a letter is pushed through my letterbox. The sight of the flap opening, then banging shut and the letter falling to the floor has the finality of a beheading. An unopened letter should be the most innocent of things. Yet I sense calamity. The worst bill. The worst abuse. The worst summons. I pick up my victim convinced that it will victimise me. The postmark's local, horribly distant or illegible. Each printed or handwritten envelope is a threat.

Every letter's a potential weapon. The suspense. The threat of abandonment – the loss of my home, my possessions and those I love around me. A letter's arrival brings a guilt that's nothing to do with its content. It spirals out into something bigger: amorphous, fantastic and absurd. I've been traced, found and seen to be wanting. In reality, it's nothing of the sort: a bill, a bank statement or a letter from a charity. The bureaucrats are simply functioning; if not like the old times.

The sheer physicality of a letter's upsetting. Fear hits me like a fist banging down on a re-used stamp. One day I'll have the courage to tear one up without having read it. Not yet though, for she might reappear: clutching that body of correspondence and bleeding on the doormat. I wished there'd been no war. That my daughter had just kept to e-mails, not those lengthy letters about her real feelings, from the territory she couldn't occupy, that awful place I enthused she should travel to.

Today I panic and often put my hand through the letterbox, hoping to grasp her hand. Touching nothing, I pull back, open the door, wanting her to return, both of us still desperate to be known.

A Further Struggle

The doctor became impatient with M who, for a seventy-five-year-old, was obscenely fit. He could do headstands. Remarkable! This amused the nurses who thought the blood would rush to M's head and that would be it – kaput! But it wasn't. He glowed from the effort. The doctor was irritated that he did it to music: an ancient record of Fred Astaire singing *Stepping Out with My Baby*. Then M put on David Bowie's *Let's Dance* and not only did a headstand but a dozen press-ups. The nurses laughed so much that the doctor and two burly helpers had to intervene. After a scuffle, M almost got the better of them.

M put one step forward. He wasn't used to exercising his legs. He was off the drugs and couldn't recall any injury or disease that had disabled him. M dimly recalled some rule, law or dictate about not walking. Was it for national security or the whim of a deranged dictator? M couldn't understand why they no longer liked you stepping out – as people once did freely in the last century.

The doctor noticed that the serum wasn't working properly. Instead of degeneration, it was causing M to experience spasms of rejuvenation. The doctor's orders were to curb the energy flow of all the elderly over-actives. Too many people like M would set a bad example to the other chronically ill people in the hospital. It was obvious to the doctor that there'd been a mistake, that the transports division had slipped up and one of the worried-well had been sent here by mistake. There were only two options left, make him ill, or send him back to be placed under home arrest. Killing was out of the question, now that the other patients had spotted him and he'd befriended the nurses.

M opened the door to fresh air. No people. No traffic. Yet wheels. Only wheels approaching. A large bicycle. No. A wheel-chair. One. Then two. Three. Four. Soon a whole procession of chairs. Empty chairs being pushed along by anxious nurses, heading towards a traffic island with people as old as M walking back and forth as if their legs had been re-born. One of the nurses spotted M. She was angry and waved her hands for him to stop. But M was on the road now, walking towards the traffic: a further struggle he could manage on his own.

The doctor hadn't expected M to want to stay in hospital. Maybe it was the effect of the drugs but his behaviour took on a strange docility. He became inert rather than ill. His dangerous excess turned in upon itself to produce a worried well-thing of a man, some lazy tamed beast. Now M told jokes and spoke in riddles about the dangerous splendour of health. They could send M anywhere, for he no longer posed a threat to the doctor whose job was to keep the populace ill. So they let him hang around the wards as a pet or court-fool, encouraging his headstands, press-ups and even a cartwheel or two.

Death of a Pig

In the Middle Ages, foxes and donkeys were put on trial. But imagine, you humans, one of your kind, tried by animals, for killing a pig.

Judge – a large bear.
Defence counsel – a farm horse.
Prosecuting counsel – a wild boar.
Defendant – a male labourer.
Clerk of the court – a wolf.
Members of the jury – various dogs, cats, pigs and chickens.

The Judge: The trial of Willard Jones, farm labourer, will commence. Read out the charge.

Clerk of the Court: Manslaughter of a pig, my lord.

Defence Counsel: I object to the term manslaughter. The victim was female.

Prosecuting Counsel: The sex of the pig is irrelevant.

Defence Counsel: Your honour, this is a case of sowslaughter.

Prosecuting Counsel: Although a sow is a lower form of species than, say, myself, a wild English boar, I consider manslaughter to be an appropriate description."

Defence Counsel: Surely if someone commits manslaughter then the person must have killed a man, or woman, of his own kind – that animal species termed human being.

Prosecuting Counsel: Given the fact that the defendant has admitted a plea of accidental killing, and not pre-meditated murder, which I intend to illustrate to the jury should be the proper charge, and we are still duty-bound to employ human legal terminology, then I believe that things should remain unaltered.

Defence Counsel: My client Mr. Willard Jones is accused of killing a pregnant sow. He did this to provide food for his wife and sick child. May I remind you of a case some twenty years ago, your honour. You will recall the affair of the infamous serial earth-worm killer. A conflict of intention arose over the fact that the female perpetrator, wearing a man's large boot, given freely by her bed-stricken husband, did stamp to death a multitude of worms on her kitchen floor. She then proceeded to the homes of her neighbours to stamp out their worms as well. The male boot, worn by a malicious female foot, was deemed a murder weapon, provided by a complicit husband, in the heinous squashing of insects. Furthermore your honour . . .

Judge: Let's get on with the trial! I suggest that we establish a neutral playing field. That the charge be changed to . . . thingslaughter!

Defence Counsel: Your honour, to do that would shame the identity of the dead pig, its relatives and the local pig community. The sow Vanessa wasn't some vague thing but a poor innocent creature, of honest character, mistakenly butchered by my client.

Defendant: It was just a pig, yer honour. I hit it ever so lightly cos it was hogging the food of the other pigs. I never meant it any harm.

Prosecuting Counsel: We have a witness. A cockerel who says you maliciously beat the sow.

Defendant: That nosey fowl hates me. She wants me put away.

And so on and so on and so on. It was half a day before the trial properly commenced. Proving that it's so difficult to put in the dock a man for accidentally killing an innocent pig – that naively believed it was, in its own right, a meaty independent sow never destined for the kitchen table of your common man or woman or perhaps the dining hall of a king.

Egg Timing

All the family enjoyed a boiled egg until father announced that he wished to be cremated.

"My ashes are to be ground down very small, put into an egg timer and sent to Margaret's family in Canada."

Janice, his younger daughter, protested. "Why can't you stay with us in Ipswich?"

"Grind me down!" ordered Father. "They retired me too early. I have to carry on working. I've spoken to the undertaker. After cremation, I want to leave a tiny bit of bone too. It'll be pulverisation by hand . . . a mortar and pestle job."

When Margaret emigrated, with her family, to Canada, Father was depressed. An accident had left him unable to walk without a stick. Once retired the ex British Aerospace worker reflected on his daughters. For five years Janice had cared for her widowed father, for as well as the walking problem he was diagnosed with diabetes. The two daughters had always been rivals for Father's love. Margaret secretly envied Janice's ability to care for the sick man. And Janice allowed no one to interfere with that skill. Yet it was Margaret, always standing to the side, in the bedroom, that Father thought more highly of.

Thrice daily, Janice made Father take his pink capsules. But the real pain was caused by Margaret's departure. Janice spoke of the thousands of miles distance between them. That it was selfish to have got up and emigrated with no warning. Janice's resentment annoyed father but once he knew he was dying, the ash idea came to him as a way to both support and spy on his daughters.

On receiving Janice's ash package, Margaret wanted to bury it in the back garden. But had second thoughts. Best honour her flaky Dad. She fastened the egg timer to the wall, near the stove, finishing the last detail in her newly installed kitchen.

"That's an old fashioned sand glass timer. When I was a kid I'd reverse the flow of sand halfway through to mess up people's eggs!" said Tony, Margaret's husband.

"Sit down, honey. Let's eat our steaks!" She gathered up a forkful of meat, raised it to her lips and hesitated. Margaret sensed she was being watched. *Always eat your greens Margaret! Wouldn't you like a boiled egg with your steak? Give me some work to do. I can't laze about the kitchen all day!* Margaret placed the fork on her plate, stood up, went over to the timer and poured out Father's ash.

"Why did you do that?" asked Tony.
"Just a whim," said Margaret.

One morning, the family desired fried eggs. So four were dutifully cracked and dropped into a pan. A revolting stench came off them. Margaret took the pan and flushed breakfast down the toilet. She returned shaken, almost as if the eggs had been outraged by their dropping into the hot oil. Tony took the remains of the carton back to the shop. They bore the correct date stamp for freshness. However, their small ends did have a strange, ashy-coloured tinge, so the manager changed them.

Margaret refused to buy more eggs. If the family wanted eggs they'd have to get their own and cook them. She wouldn't enter the kitchen until they'd been boiled, fried or poached. It was to be none of her business.

The supermarket was quiet. Margaret was reading the contents of a box of organic cornflakes, when she thought she glimpsed a man's cinerary back. Then it was gone. At the checkout, she stared at her trolley. Her chosen cereal, bread, honey and biscuits were all missing. In their place were seven cartons of eggs arranged like a cross. She went to cry out. A powdery grey hand was placed over her mouth. From a speaker came a horrible arrangement of the Beatles' *Nowhere Man*.

Back home, Margaret gripped pieces of furniture to remain calm. She kept hearing father's voice insisting that she return to cooking eggs. Margaret agreed. But it had to be on her terms.

Fried, poached, scrambled, made into omelettes: anything but boiled. Father disagreed. The eggs were cooked as she wished and the house grew quiet.

A week later, the cinerary visitation returned. At three am, Father entered Margaret's bedroom spinning like a tiny tornado to fill her wing-shaped armchair. There sat a steely dressed skeletal form with a charcoal veil of a face. In place of Father's brown eyes were grey indentations. They stared, pathetic.

"Margaret, why did you abandon me?"

"I'll keep things on the boil if that's what you want!"

"I do. Eggs, eggs! All so lovely in their way. My favourite was a duck egg. Do you remember – when you were six I sent you to Eddie's shop. You came back, with tears in your eyes, and the money. Eddie had said there'd be no more eggs on account as how the duck had died. That was a cruel thing to tell a young girl."

"Yes, it was."

"Damn his shop duck!" shouted Father.

"Why do you upset me like this, Father?"

"I had to be at your side again."

"But as ash? You ought to stay with Janice. She loves you more than me. That's where your egg timing lies."

"Janice has no family. Nothing. You've a future and things to pass on."

Margaret said nothing. Just went to the kitchen and unhooked the egg timer. She snapped its slender neck and threw it in the bin.

At dawn, a wrenching came from Margaret's wardrobe. As though something was growing. Margaret opened her eyes. Tony lay asleep beside her. His aquiline nose held in a shaft of sunlight. She affectionately ran her finger along its ridge, then squeezed the end. It was a dagger as warm as her father's beaked nose.

Cracks appeared. The door hinge was strained. The wood split. A giant egg crashed through and fell onto the white rug. Margaret got out of bed. Knelt over it. Hesitated. Then gave it a little poke. She wanted to take Tony and hammer his Daddy nose against the shell. Instead, she gently tapped it. A door opened. Inside sat Janice reading a copy of *Woman's Realm*.

"Janice, it's you. Did you get my letter?"

"Hhmm," said Janice absorbed by an article on menstruation.

"Father's just left. There's ash on the floor, but nothing to worry about!"

"Oh yes, and what did *he* have to say then?"

"Some story about eggs and me as a little girl. All such a long time ago!"

"You're lucky." Janice looked up from the magazine. "Father never told me stories. I gave him so much attention when he was ill. A story would have passed the time!"

"Didn't you mind about sending his ash over to Canada?"

"No," lied Janice. "I never fancied Dad inside an egg timer. Besides I tend to boil things by my wristwatch. Since his death, we've cut down on eggs. Cholesterol. Bad for the heart."

Margaret picked up the magazine. *Be the Omelette Queen of the Realm and Win a Super Fitted Kitchen!* was its headline. She began exploring the egg. It was sparsely furnished: a worn carpet, spider plant, bench and a table with more magazines – like an old-fashioned waiting room. Soon the great silence of the egg began to make Margaret drowsy. Both sisters (now in each other's arms) fell asleep. The egg rocked gently to and fro, as if a Humpty-Dumpty, then it smashed into a thousand smelly pieces.

Margaret showered to wash away Father and the madness. She ought to have taken her doctor's advice and made Father a little shrine. She'd get in touch with Janice. They ought to put their disagreements to one side. It had been years since they'd had a proper talk. She'd write to her this morning. Next year they could afford a trip to England. Tony was doing well at his job at the bank. She'd suggest it to him over breakfast.

The doorbell rang.

"I'll get it!" she cried.

She opened the door. There was no one there. At her feet was a letter postmarked Ipswich,

England. She was about to open it when the postman came back.

"I took this parcel next door. Sorry. It's addressed to you. You need to sign for it." The package was spherical: looking for all the world like an ostrich egg. She signed and took it in. Margaret had to ensure it was never broken.

Okura's Tree, William's Bridge

The spread of Okura's pubic hair was both wild *and* orderly. So much so that her flat stomach and strong hips dared not disturb this black winter tree. Branches of its fine wiry texture were twisted (or held down) at its thickening trunk. Whilst the ends were free and uncontained, as they branched across her skin. Pulling back Okura's skin, you exposed her thin-lipped vulva. Then the secret pubic tree became a black forest surrounding a cavern. Here the clitoris and urethra were placed in suspense if you watched too long. Okura never objected to her partner's looking but always mentally timed him. Once the territory was defined and the skin relaxed, the black embroidery of Okura's vagina remained resolutely calm.

In relation to Okura's stomach and hips, the vagina appeared a strange entity almost lying in wait. Yet waiting for what? Only when Okura's bushy tree was pressed, by fine silk or cotton underwear, was it exposed to tensions other than those directly sexual. Her pubic hair had adventures. It could be stretched and allowed to hover within the space created by Okura's bottom touching a toilet seat. After urination, it was patted by toilet tissue; brushed by the insertion of her sanitary towel; scratched if Okura itched, moistened when she chose to masturbate, and smeared with soothing creams and lotions when Okura was pained by cystitis.

A disturbing 'pleasure' sometimes arose from a woman watching her. For this act, out of Okura's control, there was nothing medicinal to treat her unease. Take a stranger standing near her as she washed her body in the public shower of a swimming pool. She sensed the European woman comparing the differences between their bodies. As Okura dried her genitalia, it became a focus of attention. The fashionable European who frequently sunbathed, wore a briefer bikini and her pubic hair was a tiny cultivated hedge compared to Okura's tree. Okura never glanced back at the stranger's genitals, nor considered her looking to be specifically erotic. She sensed that the woman wanted to touch her sex. This was done without any trace of lesbian curiosity. As if Okura were a beautiful statue whose sculptured genitalia had an intense life of its own, and should be examined for its own sake. But why the European wished to look amazed Okura, who never desired such a thing for herself. If the woman gazed too long, Okura turned so as to obscure her view, quickly finished her shower and dressed.

However, when Okura's pubic hair was observed by a man it created intrigue. To qualify, the type of man had to be Western European – more precisely an Englishman. She met William in London and he was qualified to look (Japanese males had never expressed any interest, for its own sake, in Okura's winter tree but only in probing the secret of Okura's vaginal cave.)

It's too reductive to state that women are the sex that is looked at and men the sex that does the looking. When dressed and in the public gaze, this is possibly so. Yet naked, each partner can choose to sexually survey their partner's body. The eye selects a favourite part. Be it the breasts, neck, shoulders, back, bottom or feet. If they are part of a group, then the eye settles on their most striking features. For Okura's Englishman, his group of parts was the hips, stomach, bottom, thighs and vagina. In this lower region, Okura's vagina reigned supreme. William found her pubic hair the focus of much sexual inquiry. But in the scan of William's gaze, didn't Okura sometimes imagine the glance of her former boyfriend Nagisa? Or even further back, her tentative father? Not that these previous men were intent on isolating one part of Okura's anatomy, but in their discursive and non-abusively unconscious way, were very seasoned and considerate collectors of the erotic.

The William man would like to believe he was the first to praise the Okura woman.

No, he was just the first to enthuse over her pubic hair. At first she was surprised, then amused by his interest. Maybe it was odd and naturally European to latch onto this. Okura never thought it beautiful or ugly. She would neutralize her patch so as to feel confident when William undertook his looking. Okura would part her legs; close or curl around him allowing him different views of her body. The effect was intoxicating. William couldn't resist such a calculated abandonment of flesh (time and again he returned).

Even when Okura was dressed, he'd continue to see her fine black tree. Whether she wore jeans or a dress, William had playful x-ray eyes. To him, Okura's pubic hair felt like it wanted to break through her clothes and present itself as an offering. Even when Okura wasn't there, its image coiled itself around his brain. Like a snake, it slid inside, tempted him to reach out, touch and kiss it. Dreaming of access, William had to be extra careful when driving, walking across the road or cooking a meal. Any lapse of concentration could be dangerous, erotically fatal to his system. Not because of some spurious psychoanalytical danger: that he'd be swallowed up by Okura's vagina, cast into a black sexual hole of nothingness. The danger was the threat of unity. Being too organically connected with the slit in Okura's body might mean her tree breaking into leaf; the black hair growing bigger than him and his sexual parts; a risk of deeper emotions, leading Okura to ask him difficult questions concerning the question of love.

No other part of her body, beautiful though it was, affected him in quite the same way. The western females he'd slept with had had attractive pubic hair and genitalia but this hadn't been such a turn on and was never more remarkable than their breasts, bottoms, legs or arms. William gave a great deal of attention (almost shrine worship) to this ineffable part of her.

If for William, Okura's essence lay in her vagina, then for Okura it was William's nose. It was impossible for a Japanese man to possess a European shaped nose – the physiological gulf was immense. Not big or threatening. Yet by Western cultural standards, William's nose was remarkable – long, fine and aquiline; a delicate bone encased by glistening healthy skin. However, there was an imperfection – a small bump on the bridge. It wasn't as noticeable now as when it first appeared. A cricket ball had bashed his bridge when William was fifteen. The shock and pain he'd experienced from the blow put him off sport. It also made him feel, until his early twenties, self-conscious about his nose. The first time that a woman found William's nose attractive, he was confounded. William had viewed it with distrust and frustration, a possible candidate for cosmetic surgery. But one day, everything changed. A woman said it was a good nose, even noble. Slowly William began to feel more comfortable with its shape. Later, Okura extravagantly praised it. She lovingly stroked, kissed and travelled her finger along its ridge and sides. Gradually William began to trust his nose.

Okura frequently asked him to rub his nose against her own much smaller nose. Okura never found William's nose intimidating or in danger of becoming an extra penis. Certainly in sexual play, it was the tongue, not the nose that had the right of entry to her vagina. The nose was too loveable and passively erotic to be employed for penetration. A mock duel, rub and caress of noses was sufficient sexual fun. Sometimes, because of its strength and length, William's nose would happily prod Okura's stomach or tickle her ribs. But it never ventured down to her genitals.

Okura would often dart at William to kiss and fondle his nose. One time she caused him to laugh. She'd been sitting with him, on a sofa, next to a window, pretending to read a long newspaper article, for which she had put on her glasses in order to look more serious. Her English wasn't that good. She'd pretended to read so as to impress him. In profile, William's nose, lips and chin had been snared by sunlight. Okura enjoyed his form as a beautiful composition – the calm reader, at twilight, quietly absorbed in his book. Okura noted a subtle dilation of William's nostrils accompanying a smile as he read his novel, Tolstoy's *Resurrection.* She cheekily kissed his nose. William put down his book intending to return the kiss.

But before he could, Okura determinedly pushed him back on the sofa. With his head tilted for her purpose, she pulled out her small tongue and attacked; aiming it at his nostrils. William didn't resist. This time her tongue entered his right nostril, but only briefly, for she tickled him too much. Gripping her tighter, he resisted her nosedive. Okura had to be content with kissing his chin and cheeks. He always found Okura's lips to be deliciously exciting. Her measured kisses quickly made him erect. William placed his hands on Okura's skirted bottom, hitched up her skirt and pulled off her knickers. Once the black tree was exposed, Okura didn't resist. He softly rubbed her sex till she was very excited. It felt like William was dipping his finger into a pool within the cave, so terrifically moist and hidden was she. William's fingers enjoyed probing her wetness. Every time his forefinger entered Okura's vagina, it was as if he was playing a musical instrument.

Okura made further erotic requests of his nose. That it sniff her skin, rub itself against her ribs, tap on her shoulders or stroke the nape of her neck. Sometimes William's nose and fingers became more active than his penis, sometimes not; either way it was a focal point.

William's nose and the pubic hair of Okura's genitals became the most desired parts of each other's bodies. Each read deeply from their *locus classicus*. Initially, neither had viewed these body parts as necessarily their most desirable feature. Each part grew on them (not of course literally, though that might have been strangely agreeable) till they each saw the rest of their body in a new light. All other bodily parts, whether viewed as positive or negative, were placed lower down in the hierarchy of attraction.

Before meeting Okura, William had prized his feet.

Before meeting William, Okura had prized her neck.

Ostensibly these areas were more aesthetic but a higher rudiment of desire had irrationally selected his nose and her pubic hair. Forces, they hoped, for mutual good, possibly love.

For one year they desired each other intensely. She'd never been with a European man before and he'd never been with an Asian woman. At first it was the clean excitement of opposites. A different conception of the world mirrored in their mind and body. He was lean, strong and muscular. Whilst she possessed a small, delicate, small-boned frame.

Resting, they admired, for long periods, each other's body; its overall shape, curves, irregularities, sharp edges and skin texture. The landscapes of their bodies becoming palpable countries they frequently desired to visit.

During sex, they preferred to touch more than penetrate. She loved having her neck and back stroked – this usually lead on to the rubbing of each other's genitals. When they climaxed, it was delightful. Of course, his penis frequently entered her and the predictable second coming (for both) was achieved. But orgasm could sometimes engender a sense of loss. As if they'd given up too much, too quickly, of themselves. For they always wanted to hold back a little, remain free explorative agents of sensuality. The uninhibited caress, spontaneous touch and completing embrace; when occurring on, or around the vagina and nose, proved more satisfying.

Things might have continued indefinitely (so locked were they in an erotic dream). Yet any idea of living together (they saw each other every weekend) and therefore planning for the future was constantly exiled. It was a moment by moment experience, entailing a fragile 'innocence'. Of course, they were adults, with reserves of negative sophistication, but Okura and William had a childish sense of play that overrode experience, saying that this wasn't for real and so much the better.

Whatever bonded them snapped one day without them fully realizing. Their prized objects (vagina & nose) vanished. They woke to find them missing. Who or what had removed them? If God exists, had their maker cursed them? Neither of them fully believed in God. (William had a loose 'belief' in Christian things, minus a supernatural intervention. As for Okura, she retained her childhood teaching of parental Japanese gods and goddesses on Shinto parade.)

William was the first to know. He was standing, ultimately breathing, appearing to function as if he still possessed a nose, or any semblance of a nose. More amazed than horrified, Okura couldn't summon up the words to tell him. Silently, Okura took William's arm and led him over to the bedroom mirror, where he saw the gap in his face. William's nose was defiantly missing. No bone, flesh, or anything whatsoever lingered over the spot where a fleshy protuberance had once jutted out.

Horrified, William took his hand up to the vacuum. He carefully poked his finger into the hole but couldn't feel anything. Yet he still functioned. He was standing there alive, breathing. Somehow air was inhaled and exhaled.

"William, where is your nose?" Okura's question sounded horribly absurd.

He sat down. Having just got out of bed, he and Okura were naked.

She stood back a little, looking William over. He wasn't panicking, going crazy or screaming. He just sat there confounded by the evidence. Okura wanted to kiss the nose gap, or the flesh next to it, but couldn't.

"It is like a dream. We shall wake soon and things will be back to normal," said Okura, shivering. Her top and knickers were lying where she'd left them last night, on the sofa. She put them on and left for the toilet. In the bathroom, the pain in her full bladder increased. She pulled down her knickers and glanced down at her sex.

At first she thought she looked rather bare of genitalia. She picked her glasses up from where she'd left them on the bathroom cabinet. Okura put them on and examined herself. There was a lot of sharp whiteness around her genitalia. Her pubic hair seemed to have disappeared. Why couldn't she see her sex? Was she still sleepy and in shock because of William? On the opposite wall was an enormous print by Monet of the gardens at Giverney. The lilies in the pond gently calmed her as she urinated. Consoled by Monet, she tore off a piece of tissue to dry herself.

On dabbing her body, Okura was aware that things were not right. Her anus was still intact, but when her fingers moved to her vagina, she panicked. Firstly there was no pubic hair and next no fleshy covering of the orifice. She couldn't feel a thing. When she pushed her finger into her hole, the sense of a firm, fleshy interior had vanished. Okura's finger poked round an empty cold space. She withdrew it and stared at the place her vagina had inhabited. No bone, tissue or inner body. It was now as void as the spaces where William's nose had been. Okura ran into the bedroom.

William asked Okura to feel the back of his head and confirm that the orifice, the hole in place of his nose, had not continued right through to the back. Nothing. The hole hadn't bored its way through. Likewise, Okura placed her hands around her bottom seeking a new hole but found nothing to compete with her anus or correspond to her vagina.

William stood in front of a wardrobe mirror examining his face.

"Okura, stroke my face, touch me where my nose should be." She did. Similarly William touched her sex point and acknowledged that everything was being felt but just couldn't be seen. However, when they each touched themselves they felt nothing. "What does this mean?" asked Okura. "Do you think that this is only the start . . . maybe other parts will vanish too?"

They talked, had coffee, and tried to decide what to do. They were more puzzled than frightened. Their 'missing organs' were still operative. William's 'nose' could smell the strong aroma of coffee after Okura drained her cup. Okura urinated without seeing her 'organ' work. The fact that their organs could continue doing these things without them being able to see them was reassuring. Both knew they could breathe or excrete and weren't in any immediate danger of dying. Yet what would the bigger world make of them both if other people couldn't see their anatomical parts? On this point, Okura was more fortunate than William was, as clothes hid her vagina – public showers were out and any medical inspection of her body wasn't imminent. William's predicament was more urgent. His nose was in everyday use. It was right there, in the middle of his face, for everyone to see, or now not see. A nose was essential for human intercourse. People would recoil from him if it was seen to be missing. Of course he could cover it up, bandage his face. But for how long? People would ask questions. William couldn't keep up the pretence of injury forever, nor simply hide away.

As well as concerns of a public nature, there was intimacy – the trial and experience of a couple as they sexually peaked. Yet William's rubbing of Okura's genitals and her stroking of William's nose was still possible. They could both feel the parts if not see them. But not to see them meant a lessening of excitement, a dissipation of sexual energy. A prime pleasure of sex had been the aesthetic power of those erotic bits, the alluring visual component. Could lovemaking ever be the same again?

William sat back in his chair, closed his eyes and imagined what once had been.

It would be nice to see you, nose, feel you again, he thought.

Okura looked across at him. *I miss you my sex. I need you!*

"Maybe we're being punished for over-worshipping our organs," said Okura. "We've offended the gods and now must pay for our sins!"

"Nonsense, Okura!"

"But where are they . . . who stole them?"

"I don't know."

"This has to be a bad dream."

Okura began to cry. William put his arm around her. He rubbed his invisible nose against her ear. She kissed the form of the blank space, at first gently then passionately. He touched her breast. They started fondling one another. William began to unzip his trousers. At first Okura tried to stop him. For even though he could readily feel her vagina, William's not being able to see it, at the height of his passion, might reject his visible penis. Gradually the feeling receded. William had felt no real shame about the loss of his nose, so Okura could accept her loss too. Yet if they couldn't see what they fancied could they ever be aroused in the same way? They tried hard but it wasn't the same. The highlights of their great physical state had been lost – the leisurely stroking and fingering of the pubic hair and the mad caress of the nose.

That night they dreamt of their obsessions. Yet the dream was crazy. The nose and vagina were back in their right places but it was difficult for them to stay there. They kept slipping out. It was as if they were now a bad fit (too big, too small.) Even when they appeared to fit, it wasn't for very long. They kept falling out as if they'd lost their memory, couldn't remember their function. Desperate to connect, both bits tried camping out on other parts of William and Okura. But they couldn't find a new home. Upon waking, William and Okura were very nervous.

They stopped having sex and, for the first time, talked about themselves, their lives, and their future. They allowed themselves to be gently weaned off the erotic.

This was less difficult than they'd imagined. For a life, outside of sex, was already possible – though not a fully desirable thing. They'd gone to the cinema, frequented bars, walked in the noisy park, shopped at the supermarket, exercised their laptops, phones, listened to compressed music and sat hugging one another in front of the television commercials. They had shared but not really shared anything. Okura and William hadn't discussed or planned a future. Any life of the future was too big, too awkward, too unnecessary to consider. So much was based in the present moment of the limpid nose and pliant vagina. William had walked across the bridge to find Okura's tree. Okura had grown her roots to tickle William's bridge.

It took a further week of dreaming, talking and assessing before the nose and vagina returned. Of course they rejoiced when things were back to normal. They'd moved on, not necessarily matured, but fractionally developed. Now other parts of their bodies felt equally important for their sexual curiosity. William and Okura re-commenced lovemaking but it was never quite the same. Gradually the interest in the body shifted. The allure of the breast, bottom, stomach and penis – came to stand, in line, behind their growing feelings. The heart of Okura and William became the new passionate binding force. Okura and William had authentically fallen in love.

At first they were scared. This was a shift of focus and attention. They didn't want the heart itself to physically disappear. The removal of that organ would have meant the couple's removal. And the heart was not something they wanted to prove by physically seeing. The incision, of a surgeon's knife, would reveal the evidence. Yet such a cut was madness. For then all the organs would be closer to death and love would cease. Especially for Okura's tree and William's bridge, still very much alive at the edges, patiently hiding their old desire, lying in wait to return to the country of flesh and bone.

The Richter Scale

Stop laughing . . . the condom might fall off or burst . . . don't shake your body . . . I think we'll explode the bed . . . us, the room . . . the house . . . London . . . all this giggling and tremors . . . too much tonight on the Richter scale . . . don't shriek and bounce so . . . my penis doesn't get the joke . . . nor do I . . . look, I know sex can be absurd . . . my organ wanting to get to know your organ . . . the technical fiasco that can happen . . . but things were going fine . . . we fitted well enough . . . now all this noise . . . movement . . . please . . . it will all end in tears . . . such belly laughing madness . . . the big rock will roll down into the sea!

She laughed till she came and he didn't. He took everything out that was his and what belonged to the waste bin – their condom of shook-up sperm.

Post-coital giggles echoed through her.

Cool as a stone the woman

   s

     a

       n

        k

          into

            her

              pillow.

Alan Price lives in London. He is a poet, scriptwriter, short story writer, film critic for the online *Filmuforia* and blogger at alanprice69.wordpress.com. His short story collection *The Other Side of the Mirror*, an alternative take on vampirism, was published by Citron Press in 1999. A TV film *A Box of Swan* was broadcast on BBC 2 in 1990. Alan has scripted five short films. The last one *Pack of Pain* (2010) won four international film festival awards. His debut collection of poetry *Outfoxing Hyenas* was published by Indigo Dreams in 2012. A pamphlet of prose poems *Angels at the Edge* (Tuba Press) appeared in 2016. The poetry chapbook, *Mahler's Hut* was published in 2017 by Original Plus Books. And his latest poetry book is the 2018 *Wardrobe Blues for a Japanese Lady* (The High Window Press). Alan is currently writing a novel and also working on a series of prose poems based on films with the working title *The Cinephile Poems*.